Emma Dilemma and the New Nanny

Dad

McClain

Annie

Emma

Lizzie + Ira

Tim

Mom

Emma Dilemma and the New Nanny

by Patricia Hermes

Marshall Cavendish

For Benjamin and Suad, with love

Marshall Cavendish Corporation
99 White Plains Road
Tarrytown, NY 10591
www.marshallcavendish.us

Library of Congress Cataloging-in-Publication Data
Hermes, Patricia.
Emma Dilemma and the new nanny / by Patricia Hermes.
p. cm.
Summary: Emma tries to help her parents understand that, although their beloved new nanny has made a few mistakes, no one can behave perfectly responsibly all the time.
ISBN-13: 978-0-7614-5286-7
ISBN-10: 0-7614-5286-9
[1. Responsibility—Fiction. 2. Family life—Fiction. 3. Nannies—Fiction. 4. Ferrets as pets—Fiction.] I. Title.
PZ7.H4317Emm 2006
[Fic]—dc22
2005024668

The text of this book is set in Souvenir.
Book design by Adam Mietlowski

Printed in The United States of America
First edition
10 9 8 7 6 5 4 3 2 1

 **Marshall Cavendish** Children

Table of Contents

Chapter One
Marmaduke Is Missing

"Psst! Tim!" Emma whispered.

She stood outside her brother's door, looking in at the lump in the bed. Tim always slept with the covers over his head. Even though he was a year older—ten months and two weeks to be exact—he wasn't brave like she was. He was scared of things, like monsters that came out at night, even though he said he knew there were no such things.

Emma shifted from foot to foot. She wished she had put her frog slippers on. Her feet felt as cold as Popsicles. She waited a moment more, watching Tim. Across the room, she could see the screen saver on his computer. It looked as if it were shipping fishes off the screen and out to sea, then rounding them up again. It made her feet feel even colder.

Should she go in? They had a deal—she wouldn't go into his room, and he wouldn't go into hers without asking. But Marmaduke, her pet ferret, was missing. So forget about that deal. She tiptoed in and sat on his bed. "Hey!" she whispered. "Wake up."

He didn't.

She leaned over and blew in his face.

Tim sat up. "It's dark!" he said.

"Duh! It's night!" Emma said. "But guess what? Marmaduke's gone."

Tim flopped back on his pillow. He shut his eyes. "Wait 'til morning, okay? The new nanny is coming. She'll help find him."

"Unh-uh," Emma said. "Remember what happened with the last nanny? She thought Marmaduke was a rat and tried to squash him with a shovel. Besides, Mom said if he gets in trouble anymore, he's going back to the pet shop. Pronto! That means quick."

Tim was breathing deep again.

"Tim, come on!" Emma said.

Tim sat up. "What if he's in Ira's bed like last time?"

"He's not," Emma said. She sure hoped that was true. Ira was their baby brother, a twin to Lizzie. Marmaduke had leapt into Ira's crib one night and nibbled on the toes of his footy pajamas. Marmaduke didn't mean to hurt Ira or anything. But Ira woke up screaming, and then Lizzie began screaming. That woke up their sister McClain. Then Woof started barking. Mom said if it hadn't been the middle of the night, she'd have taken Marmaduke back to the pet store that very minute. Pronto.

"He didn't get his supper tonight. I went to feed him, and he was gone," Emma said. "I bet he's in the kitchen having cereal. Like last time."

"Or eating my Pop Tarts like that other time," Tim said, grumpy sounding.

"He only ate one," Emma said. "Now be really quiet, okay? Mom and Daddy just went to bed."

Tim made a face, but he got up. The computer screen threw off just enough light for Emma to see him slide his feet into his slippers. She was jealous. She didn't want to get her slippers from her room, though, because Tim might go back to sleep.

Tim put on his bathrobe.

3

He tied his bathrobe.

He picked up his flashlight from his bedside table.

"Tim!" Emma said. "Hurry up!"

"I'm coming! But we can't turn on any lights, so we'll need the flashlight."

"I know, but Marmaduke could chew through the wall and be a mile away by the time you're ready."

"He couldn't run a mile that fast. Besides, I'll just be a minute," Tim said. Then he took two whole, entire minutes to flip the flashlight on and off, checking that it worked.

Emma shook her head. Tim was so organized, it was scary. Sometimes Emma wished she was just a teeny weeny bit like him—like right now. She could hardly feel her feet anymore.

"Are you ready?" she asked.

"Ready," Tim said.

Together, they tiptoed into the hall and down the stairs. They knew the steps to skip: the third from the top, the third from bottom, and the bottom one. Those steps creaked. Well, actually, all the steps creaked, because the house was really old. But some of them creaked more than others.

At the bottom, Emma stopped to listen. The last time Marmaduke had escaped to the kitchen, they had heard him from the hall crunching on the cereal. Now, though, there was no sound at all. The hall was very, very dark and very, very quiet.

"Let's go," Emma whispered, and she started off for the kitchen.

At the kitchen door, she turned around. Tim was still standing at the foot of the stairs. He had his flashlight on, but it was only a penlight one, so it was very dim.

"Tim!" Emma whispered.

"I don't hear him," Tim said. "Let's go back to bed."

Emma knew what was wrong. She walked over to Tim and took his hand.

Together they tiptoed down the hallway to the kitchen. They crept across the room to the pantry. Emma pushed open the door. There was a light switch on the wall by the door. She flicked it on. She blinked.

Cereal. Crackers. Rows of soup. Jars of peanut butter and jams and pasta.

No Marmaduke.

Emma wrapped her arms around herself.

"Remember the time we found him in the cellar?" she asked.

"No way!" Tim said. "Not me."

"I know," Emma said. "I didn't mean we should look down there."

Actually, she did mean that. But she didn't *really* want to go down to the cellar either. It was dark and spidery. One time she walked right into a spider web, and it got stuck in her hair. She never did find out where the spider went. For a long time afterward, she kept thinking she felt it in her ear.

"Let's go back to bed," Tim said.

"But I need him!" Emma said.

"Are you really taking him to school tomorrow?" Tim asked.

Emma sighed. "If I find him. I promised everybody. Even Mrs. Adams thought it would be a great report." She switched off the light, and Tim took her hand.

Together they went back upstairs, being careful to skip those creaky steps. A nightlight shone dimly in the upstairs hall. No light came from under the door in Mom and Daddy's room. That meant they were both asleep.

"Let's check the twins' room," Emma whispered.

Tim nodded.

They tiptoed to the babies' room. Tim shone the flashlight into the cribs. Ira was lying on his back, his arms above his head, flat as a shadow. Lizzie was sleeping face-down, her knees pulled up under her, her bottom up in the air.

But no Marmaduke.

"McClain's room next," Emma whispered.

They crept down the hall to McClain's room and opened the door. McClain was their middle sister and loved animals even more than Emma did. Emma sometimes thought McClain was really a dog disguised as a kid. Tim shone the flashlight in. Woof, the family's huge standard poodle, looked up at them from the foot of McClain's bed. His ears perked up.

"Hush!" Emma said to him, as Tim pulled the door shut. There was no way that Marmaduke could be in McClain's room, not with Woof there. There would have been barking and chasing and galumphing all over the place.

They tiptoed past Mom and Daddy's door. Then they heard it—the sound of feet hitting the floor. The sound of Mom shouting.

"It's alive!" she yelled.

"The mattress!" Daddy said.

"Something's in the mattress," Mom said. "It's—it's alive!"

Tim looked at Emma.

Emma looked at Tim.

"Uh oh," Emma said.

Chapter Two
Marmaduke Escapes. Again.

The next morning at breakfast, everyone was "out of sorts." That's what Mom said. She meant they were grumpy. Emma grinned. "I'm not out of sorts," she said. "I have plenty of sorts."

Mom gave her a look.

Emma dropped her eyes. She tried hard not to smile. She knew she had to be extra good. Last night, it had taken a long time to coax Marmaduke out of the mattress. Mom said they'd have to have a "talk" in the morning. Emma was afraid she knew what that meant—that Marmaduke was on his way back to the pet shop. That made her stomach ache. She had lain awake a long time making a list in her head of why Mom should give Marmaduke another chance.

Emma had another worry this morning. Because she was taking Marmaduke to school for her report, she had to sneak him out of the house. She hadn't told Mom about taking him because she was pretty sure Mom would say no. But if Mom didn't know about it, then she couldn't actually *say* no. So Emma wouldn't really be disobeying. She planned to hide Marmaduke in her backpack. Often, Mom checked it for her homework and lunch. So Emma decided she'd rush upstairs right before the bus came, pretending she'd forgotten something. She'd tuck Marmaduke in her backpack, wait 'til the bus driver beeped, run downstairs, and dash out the door. It would be tricky. If she got caught, Mom and Daddy would never allow her to be on the traveling soccer team. And that was something else for Emma to worry about. She wanted the traveling soccer team almost more than anything she had ever wanted in her life. She loved soccer, *loved* it.

The only ones who weren't grouchy this morning were the twins. They were happily eating applesauce and yogurt—with their hands—and jabbering away to one another. Even though they had just turned two years old, they could say just about everything.

Daddy was *really* grouchy. "How can two little people make such a huge mess?" Daddy said, looking at the twins.

"I'm not yittle," Ira said. "I'm two!"

"I'm three and a half," Lizzie said, smiling up at Daddy.

"You are not three and a half," Daddy said. "You are two years old, both of you, and you are making a great, big mess."

"You're just tired, honey," Mom said.

"You can count on that!" Daddy said.

Emma felt bad. She knew Daddy was tired from chasing Marmaduke last night. And now he was leaving for five days, piloting a plane to Europe and back. It was important that pilots be rested before taking a plane up in the sky. Emma hoped he had a copilot whose children and pets had slept all night.

Tim wasn't grumpy, just quiet, but McClain made up for him in grumpiness. "Me and Woof could've catched Marmaduke easy!" she told Emma. "Why didn't you wake us up? That was mean!" She stuck out her lip.

"It wasn't mean. And don't have a tantrum!" Emma said.

McClain glared at Emma. McClain had lots of tantrums. The other day, she had a king-sized one in the middle of the mall. She had wanted Mom to buy her a bathing suit, and when Mom said it was too cold for bathing suits, she threw herself down on the floor. People had to step around her. "Just the terrible twos," Mom told everybody, sort of embarrassed looking. But McClain wasn't two years old anymore. She was almost five, and Emma didn't think she was improving any with age.

The person who was most out of sorts, though, was Mom. The new nanny was coming, and she was supposed to arrive before they left for school. Mom always got manic when they got a new nanny. She worried herself to pieces, hoping the nanny would like them. But after a little while, Mom didn't like the nanny anymore and sent her away. Then they had to start all over again.

The good thing was that so far, Mom hadn't said anything more about a "talk," maybe because she was thinking about the nanny. Still, Emma ate her cereal quietly, without slurping. She finished off her orange juice without wiping her mouth on her sleeve. She said "please" and "thank you," a whole lot. Just once, she couldn't resist making a mustache. She held a crust of bread under her nose with her puffed-out lips. When Mom turned to her, she pretended to be licking jam off the toast. *Be good!* she reminded herself. *Pretend that you're Tim.*

Ira squiggled himself up in his highchair. He teetered back and forth. "Down," he said, holding out his arms.

"Down, *please?*" Mom said, reaching to steady him.

"Down, *peas!*" Ira said.

"Just a minute," Mom said. "I have to wipe your hands."

"I did," Ira said.

"You did?" Mom said. "How?"

"On my hair," Ira said. "See?" He held out his clean hands.

Daddy groaned. Mom just sighed and pushed her chair back from the table.

Emma jumped up. "I'll do it, Mom!" she said. "I'll get the washcloth."

She hurried out to the kitchen, ran the water, wet the washcloth, and squeezed it out. Then she scooted back to the dining room.

Daddy and Tim were bent over the schedule for the plane trip. Tim was tracing the map with his finger. Tim loved maps.

"See?" Daddy said to Tim. "Ireland. Right off the English coast."

Mom still had one hand out, steadying Ira, but she, too, was looking toward the map.

"You can let go, I have him, Mom," Emma said. She turned to Ira. "Here you go, buddy." She washed his little face, and he grabbed the washcloth with his teeth. "Let go, rascal," she said.

He did. Then he put his arms up for Emma to lift him out.

She lifted him, set him down, and then turned to Lizzie.

"I'll do Lizzie, too," Emma said.

Nobody seemed to hear her.

Lizzie's face was an applesauce-and-yogurt mess. Emma washed her face, but it wasn't easy. Lizzie kept turning her head back and forth, trying to escape.

"Yuck!" Emma said. She decided for the millionth time that she'd never have kids. When she was finished with Lizzie, she helped Lizzie down and looked at Mom. Everyone was still bent over the map, even McClain who couldn't read yet. Emma waited for someone to notice how good she'd been. *See, Mom, see how responsible I am? I could be on the traveling soccer team and not get in trouble. And I'm going to start taking extra good care of Marmaduke. You'll see.* But nobody noticed how wonderful she'd been. So she said, "Mom! I washed both babies. Mom!"

"Thanks, Emma," Mom said. She didn't look up from the map. "See, Tim? This is where Daddy's going to be."

Daddy was drawing a line for Tim, showing him the route of his plane. If Tim knew exactly where Daddy was, then he didn't worry so much. But Emma knew he still worried a little.

Now that the twins were set free, they decided to tackle Woof. Ira grabbed his neck, while Lizzie grabbed his stubby tail. Woof barked and circled wildly, with the twins hanging on. All that, just as the doorbell rang.

Mom looked up. She ran a hand through her mop of hair. She swept toast crumbs off the table. She reached a hand out for Daddy. "That's her!" she said. "The new nanny!"

Chapter Three
Annie Nanny

"It's okay, Sweets!" Dad said, patting her arm. "It's just a nanny. We've had dozens."

"But first impressions count for so much!" Mom said. She hurried to the hall door and opened it. "Good morning, Annie O'Reilly!" she said. "Come in, come in, please! The children can't wait to meet you. We're in the dining room."

Mom dropped her voice, then, and spoke some more. The nanny said something. They spoke together for another moment or two. Then Mom came back to the dining room, the nanny at her side.

"Everybody!" Mom said, with that extra cheerful voice she used sometimes. "Say hello to Annie O'Reilly."

Everybody looked up. Daddy stood and smiled. They all studied Annie O'Reilly. Even Woof.

This was a nanny!? She didn't look at all like nannies usually looked. All the other nannies had been round and short and plain and horribly old looking. They'd worn fat-faced watches and flat-heeled shoes, and Mrs. Corcoran, the last one, had worn bedroom slippers because of her corns. But Annie O'Reilly was young and tall and pretty and as thin as a stick. She wore her jeans rolled up, and she had on red, high-top sneakers. Her earrings dangled almost to her shoulders, and her lips were glosssed with bright, pink lipstick. Her curly, red hair streamed out from under a hat, the kind of hat actors wore in old movies. Annie was definitely the most beautiful person Emma had ever seen, even more beautiful than the Disney princesses.

"Hi, Annie," Emma said in her most polite voice. She looked at Mom.

Mom smiled at her, then turned to the other children. "We're all so happy to meet Annie, aren't we, children? Say hello."

"No," Ira said.

"Hi," Lizzie said.

McClain scowled. She didn't say anything.

Mom pulled out a chair for Annie. "Please sit

down," she said. "I've taken the day off to be with you today. Now, as you know from our interview, I head the restoration committee for the museum. It's supposed to be a nine-to-five job, but some days, it's nine 'til nine. My husband is a pilot, so he's often away. He's leaving today, in fact."

"For Ireland, and Tim doesn't want him to go," McClain interrupted. "And we are not allowed in Mom's office."

"Right," Mom said. "That's strictly off-limits. Oh, and that's Woof," she said, as Woof sidled up to Annie and began sniffing at her. "Just ignore him."

"He's a dog!" Ira said.

Annie smiled. "I can see that." When she smiled, her teeth stuck out a little, but it was a sweet smile. She patted Woof, who put his head in her lap.

"The children have busy schedules, too," Mom went on, "though we try not to over-schedule them. Monday, McClain has dance class and Tim has computer class. Tuesday, Lizzie and Ira have gymnastics. Thursday, there's soccer practice for Emma and flute lessons for Tim." Mom paused. She looked at Daddy, her eyebrows raised. Daddy made his face blank.

Mom turned back to Nanny. "At the children's music school, we like to dress up a bit," she said.

Annie smiled. "Sure, and I'll wear a suit on those days, if you prefer," she said. Her voice was soft and had a little lilt to it, almost like she was singing the words. Irish, Emma decided. Annie O'Reilly was Irish. She sounded exactly like McClain's dance teacher who taught Irish clogging.

"Oh, that would be lovely!" Mom said. "Though of course, you look fine right now. Just perfect for playing with the children. Now about the children's school schedules. Every Wednesday, Emma has a report due with a presentation . . ."

Mom stopped and turned to Emma. "Today's Wednesday!"

Emma's shoulders drooped. Didn't Mom ever forget anything?

"What did you prepare?" Mom asked.

Emma tried to keep her eyes wide and not look away. She made herself not blush. Well, she tried not to blush. It didn't work, though, she could tell. Her face got very hot. "A report," she said. "But I'm not taking anything. I mean, just a, you know, a thing about ferrets."

"A *thing* about ferrets?" Mom said. "What kind of thing?"

"I know!" McClain piped up. "Take Marmaduke. Annie, I mean, Nanny, I mean . . . I mean, Marmaduke got loose last night, and they didn't wake me up and . . ."

"Hush," Emma said. "I'm not taking Marmaduke. You can't show something live in your presentation."

She looked at Mom. It was only a little lie. The real rule was you could only bring in something live *once*, and today was Emma's once.

"What's the 'thing' on ferrets?" Mom asked.

"A report," Emma said. "I did a report. With really, really good research."

That wasn't a lie. She had done a whole lot of real research on what it was like to own a ferret.

"Oh," Mom said. "Well, that sounds good."

"And I just remembered!" Emma said. She jumped up. "I didn't put it in my backpack yet."

She ran upstairs. Now, if Mom would just stay busy with Annie, Emma could sneak Marmaduke outside in her backpack. She ran into her room, picked up her backpack, and bent over Marmaduke's cage.

The cage top was open. The books Emma

had used to weigh it down were scattered all about. And Marmaduke was gone.

Her heart pounded wildly. Suddenly, Woof began to bark. The twins began squealing. Emma ran out in the hall just as Woof came bounding up the stairs—chasing Marmaduke. Annie was running after them both. Mom was at the foot of the steps yelling, "Emma!"

"Woof, stop!" Emma yelled.

She swatted at Woof, then dove toward Marmaduke. She almost cracked heads with Annie who had just made a flying leap onto Marmaduke. Annie lay flat out on the floor, her hat tilted sideways, Marmaduke squeezed to her chest.

For a moment, Emma and Annie just looked at one another.

"What shall I do with him?" Annie whispered.

"Hold on," Emma whispered. "I'll get my backpack." She called downstairs, "We got him, Mom. He's not hurt or anything."

"Oh, wonderful!" Mom said back.

"Don't worry, I won't let him go," Annie whispered.

Emma hurried into her room, got her back-pack, and brought it to the hall. Annie had struggled to her feet and was holding Marmaduke tightly but gently. Together, they slid Marmaduke into the backpack.

"I'll get some duct tape later," Annie said. "We'll fix that cage." She snapped the buckles of the backpack. She left just enough room for Marmaduke's head to peep out through the top. "In Ireland, I had a little pig I used to carry around, just like this," she said softly, as she handed the backpack to Emma.

"You lived in Ireland?" Emma said.

"That I did. Me whole life," Annie said. "He's sweet, this wee one, isn't he?"

The school bus beeped outside.

"He is," Emma said. "But please don't tell Mom I'm taking him to school. I'll explain later." She smiled at Annie. "See you!" she said.

Annie smiled back. "See you," she answered.

Emma turned and bounded down the stairs, almost colliding with Tim who was heading for the door. "Bye, Mom," Emma shouted. "Bye, Daddy! Bye, Annie!"

Outside, she raced for the bus, her backpack tight against her chest. She had Marmaduke. She had her report ready. And at last, she had a nanny who liked ferrets.

Chapter Four

The Bite

At school, everyone crowded around Emma, wanting to hold Marmaduke. Emma said no. She didn't want to spoil her presentation by letting anyone hold him now.

"Oh, but he's so cute!" Molly said. "Can't I hold him for just a minute, please?"

"No," Emma said, holding Marmaduke close. "Not 'til later."

"How come he's not black?" Sydney said. "Ferrets are supposed to be black."

"They are not. Not all of them," Emma said. "Marmaduke's silver."

"He's not silver. He's gray!" Jordan said. He tried to grab Marmaduke right out of Emma's arms. "Just for a minute!" he said.

"Just one minute! My brother has a ferret and I know all about how to hold him, and . . ."

"No! Stop it!" Emma said. She twisted away from Jordan, holding Marmaduke high above her head. His little feet scrabbled in the air, and he made snuffly sounds.

"Emma! Jordan!" Mrs. Adams said. "Settle down. Emma, put your ferret in Puffy's cage, right now, please."

Emma did, feeling just a little sad. Puffy had been the class rabbit until he ran away. He had escaped into the woods when Emma was looking after him during the summer.

With Marmaduke safely in the cage, Emma felt relieved—and excited. Her presentation time was right after computer class, and she could hardly wait. Marmaduke, though, didn't seem a bit excited. In fact, he acted kind of bored with school. Emma didn't really blame him. Anyway, she knew that he'd perk up once she took him out of his cage later.

As soon as the morning songs and the Pledge of Allegiance were over, it was time for computer class. Emma hurried to the computer station next to Jordan. Even though he was mean, he was really good with computers, and

Emma needed his help. She hated computers a really lot.

"Jordan?" Emma whispered. "When we're finished, will you help me save my documents?"

"You wouldn't let me hold Marmaduke."

"I know. But he had to sleep. I'll let you hold him when I show the class."

"I get to hold him first then," Jordan said.

Emma nodded.

"And longest," Jordan added.

"Okay," Emma said. "Longest, too. Does your brother really have a ferret?"

"Yeah, but he never lets me play with him."

"That's mean," Emma said. She thought about Tim. She always let her brother play with Marmaduke. "How come?"

Jordan shrugged. "I guess 'cause I dropped him once."

"Emma? Jordan? Are you talking?" Mrs. Adams said. She came up to their computer station. "You know the rule. No talking during computer class."

Emma looked away. She felt her face get hot.

"Did you forget?" Mrs. Adams asked.

"*I* didn't," Jordan said.

"Oh?" Mrs. Adams said.

"I mean, *I* wasn't talking," Jordan said.

"Well, both of you be quiet now," Mrs. Adams said.

When Mrs. Adams walked away, Emma made a face at Jordan, then started on her haiku poetry. Haiku poetry meant they had to learn all about syllables and lines. It was kind of fun. Emma worked on a haiku about mean Jordan, and before she knew it, computer class was over. Since Jordan had been such a pain, her best friend, Luisa, helped her save her poem to the computer, and then to her own disk.

As soon as everyone was settled, it was time for Emma's presentation. The rule was that each presentation had to be not only fun, but educational as well. That's because Mrs. Adams said that they weren't little kids anymore. Emma had practiced and studied a lot.

She went to the front of the room and carefully lifted Marmaduke out of his cage. He looked sort of surprised.

"Hi, Buddy," she whispered. "Remember? We're in school. Be on your best behavior, all right?"

She turned to the class. "This is Marmaduke," she said. "He's a ferret. He's very playful, very fun, and he's smarter than a dog or a cat. He's a cousin of a weasel and a skunk, but he's not a rat."

She shifted Marmaduke around to face the class. "See how cute he is?" she said. "He's a domesticated ferret, not a wild one, and there's a difference."

"What difference?" Morgan called out.

"I'll take questions in a minute," Emma answered. She kind of liked saying that. It made her feel like a teacher.

She moved Marmaduke to her shoulder. He snuggled up against her neck, looking out at the class. "Domestic ferrets have been domesticated for almost three thousand years!" she went on. "That means they live with people, in houses, and not, like, wild. Some people don't like the way ferrets smell. There's a way to keep ferrets from smelling bad: Don't give them a lot of baths. That sounds weird, but it's true. Baths do something to their fur, and it makes them smell bad. You have to clean their cages a lot, though, and change the litter. They like to run around free for lots of hours in a day. They'll even play with your other pets, like your dog or cat. I have a dog, Woof. His real name is Fritz, but everybody calls him Woof 'cause that's what the twins called him when they first learned to talk. Marmaduke likes Woof. Sometimes, they sleep right next to each other. Sometimes, though, Woof chases Marmaduke, and I have to stop him. Woof wouldn't hurt Marmaduke on purpose. But Woof is super big. He's so big he can rest his head right on the table. If he caught Marmaduke in his mouth, he might kill him by accident. Ferrets like to burrow in things. Last night, Marmaduke got inside my mom and dad's mattress. He steals things and hides them. Once, he stole my dad's pen. We found it behind the couch. The end." She looked around. "Now, I'll take questions."

"Can I hold him *now*?" Molly asked.

"I go first," Jordan said.

Emma just squinted at him. No way! He had lied about not talking before. Besides, he hadn't helped with the computer at all.

"Does he bite?" Matthew asked.

"Sometimes," Emma said, sliding a look at Jordan. "He nibbles sometimes."

"That was a lovely presentation, Emma,"

Mrs. Adams said. "Now why don't you let everyone come up and take turns holding him? Children, you can line up in a straight line and hold Marmaduke one at a time. Remember to be gentle."

Everybody lined up. Emma handed Marmaduke to one kid after the other. When it was Jordan's turn, Emma put Marmaduke in his hands. Marmaduke squirmed, whipping his head around and around.

"Hey! He's trying to get away!" Jordan said. He closed his hands around Marmaduke tightly.

"Not so tight!" Emma said.

"Ow!" Jordan yelled suddenly. He threw his hands up into the air and let Marmaduke go.

Emma had been hovering over Jordan. She snatched Marmaduke before he fell to the floor.

"He bit me!" Jordan yelled, as Mrs. Adams came rushing to his side.

Emma looked at Jordan. A drop of blood bubbled up on Jordan's finger. When he wiped it on his pants, it bubbled right back up again.

"Uh-oh," Mrs. Adams said. "I think you'd better go to the nurse's office. Miguel, you go with him." She turned to Emma. "Let's put Marmaduke back in his cage, all right?"

"He didn't mean to bite," Emma explained. "It's just that Jordan was squeezing the guts out of him."

"I know he didn't mean to, Emma," Mrs. Adams said. She opened the top of Puffy's cage so Emma could set Marmaduke inside. "Animals just do that sometimes. But I'm going to send a note home to Jordan's mother and also to yours."

"You can't!" Emma wailed. "Marmaduke didn't do it on purpose!"

"I know," Mrs. Adams said, putting a hand lightly on Emma's shoulder. "And I'm sure that Marmaduke has had all his shots. But Jordan's mother will probably want to see proof of that. That's all. Now go sit down. There's nothing to worry about."

Emma went and sat down. She glared at Mrs. Adams. Nothing to worry about? When Mom didn't know that she'd brought Marmaduke to school? Mom would surely act on her threat to send him back to the pet store. And there went Emma's chance of getting on that traveling soccer team, too. If only Jordan hadn't tried to squeeze him to death. Marmaduke was just defending himself. But would Mom believe that? Would Mom even care? Emma didn't think so. She was even a little mad at Marmaduke. Why did he have to go and bite Jordan? Emma put her chin on her fists and made mad faces. How was she going to find a way out of this new dilemma?

Chapter Five
Annie to the Rescue

When Emma got off the bus, she had Marmaduke and a note from the school nurse, Miss Thompson, in her backpack. Miss Thompson wanted Mom to send a copy of the vet's certificate to school. The school needed proof that Marmaduke had had all his shots. Now Mom would definitely find out that Marmaduke had gone to school.

"Don't worry, Emma," Tim said, as they started up the front walk. "Mom won't find out. We can find the vet's papers ourselves."

"How?" Emma asked. She shifted her backpack to her chest. Marmaduke's little head was sticking out, and he was looking all around. She pushed him down, gently, and zipped up the backpack all the way. "I'll let you out in a minute, buddy," she whispered to him.

"We look through Mom's desk, that's how," Tim said. "You know how organized she is. I bet she even has a file labeled 'Marmaduke.'"

"Yeah," Emma said. "A file labeled Marmaduke with a list of all the times he's escaped. And her desk is in her office and it's off-limits! I'll just take Marmaduke and run away."

"You will not," Tim said.

"No," Emma said. "But I'm not giving up Marmaduke, either. Tim, if Mom is in the hall when we go in, just tell her I really, really, really have to go to the bathroom. I can run upstairs with Marmaduke then, okay?"

"Okay," Tim said, as he pulled open the front door. "Run!"

No one was in the hall. But Emma raced up the stairs and into her room anyway, slamming the door behind her. She leaned back against the door. Safe.

"Okay, Marmaduke," she whispered, undoing the backpack and lifting him out. "Time to go back in your house."

She looked around. Things looked different.

It was Emma's job to clean her room, but somebody else had made her bed. And things were picked up and . . .

And Marmaduke's cage was gone! Mom had taken it away. Marmaduke was going back to the store. Emma held Marmaduke close to her chest, tears filling her eyes.

"It's all right, buddy," she whispered, swallowing hard. "If you have to leave, I'm going with you." She opened the door to her room. "Mom!" she shouted. "Where's the cage? Why did you . . . ?"

She raced down the front stairs, almost knocking over Tim who was running up.

"Emma!" Tim said. "Come on. Annie wants you."

"No!" Emma cried. "Where's Mom? Marmaduke's cage is gone."

"It's okay!" Tim said. "Come on!"

"It's not okay!" Emma said.

"It is!" Tim said. "Come!" He motioned her to the back hall by the kitchen. A set of curvy stairs led up to a little apartment on the third floor. It's where the nannies lived if they wanted to. Some of the nannies had lived in. Some couldn't wait to go home at night.

Emma shook her head. "I'm not going," she said. "I want Mom! She can't send Marmaduke back."

"Emma!" Tim said. "Will you listen? Annie has a surprise for you."

"What kind of surprise?" Emma asked, warily.

"Come on," Tim said. "You'll see. It's all right."

Emma followed Tim up the back stairs, still clutching Marmaduke to her chest. There at the top were Ira and Lizzie and McClain and Annie inside a tent made out of blankets. Ira had a crown on his head, one of those things from Burger King. Lizzie had lipstick smeared all over her face. McClain was twirling around, one hand holding a Tinker Toy like it was a wand, pretending to be a dancer or a fairy, maybe. She was wearing her bikini bathing suit that she wore every chance she got—even though Mom insisted that it was getting too cold for that. Woof was stretched out on his side, half asleep, but with one eye opening once in a while. And in the center of the circus tent was a cage, much bigger and fancier than Marmaduke's. It had three rooms, like mini cages, attached to it. Lizzie's old stuffed tiger was inside the cage.

"Hi, Emma!" Annie said. "Marmaduke keeps escaping because he's bored. He won't get bored now. I got a fine, strong lock, too."

"But how . . . ?" Emma asked. "I mean . . . I mean, where's Mom?"

"Your mum's in her office," Annie said. "Somebody called from the museum with an emergency. She had to do some e-mail. She'll be finished soon, she said."

"In *two minutes!*" Ira said. He held up two fingers and nodded so hard the little crown on his head wobbled.

Lizzie straightened his crown.

"So why's the cage up here?" Emma asked. "What did you do with the old one?"

"Well," Annie said. "When we went for our afternoon walk, the little ones just had to go to the pet store, you know? And there was a sale on cages! So we came back and got the old cage and made a trade. This new one cost almost nothing. So then we decided to have a circus day. The little tiger here was the star. Now that Marmaduke's back, he can be the star. When I had me little pig, me sisters and me had circus days all the time. We even dressed up our pig in dresses."

"Oh," Emma said, because she couldn't think of anything else to say. And then she said, "Thank you."

Chapter Six
Marmaduke's New Home

Gently, Emma lowered Marmaduke into the cage. Woof got up and sniffed at Marmaduke's butt. Emma elbowed Woof aside. "This is a very cool cage!" Emma said, looking up at Annie.

Annie smiled.

"I carried it home," Ira said.

"Did not!" McClain said. "I did."

"I helped," Ira said.

"I did," Lizzie said.

"You all helped," Annie said. "You were grand!"

"I helped most!" McClain said.

"I couldn't have done it without a one of you," Annie said, putting out a hand and ruffling McClain's hair.

McClain ducked away.

"Look!" Tim said. "Marmaduke likes it."

Tim was right. Marmaduke was sniffing around, making his way in and out of his little apartment rooms. Emma thought that maybe he would be more content now. And if he didn't escape so much, Mom would be happy. But then Emma remembered The Bite.

"Annie?" she said. "The school nurse wants Marmaduke's papers."

"The nurse? Papers?" Annie asked.

"Yes, you know. Like about his shots and all."

"Why?"

Emma looked over at Tim. "Marmaduke got in a little trouble today," she said.

"Not really *trouble*," Tim said.

"He bit somebody, I bet," McClain said.

"Did not!" Emma said. "Well, maybe he did, but it was just a little bite. Could you get his vet papers from Mom's desk, Annie? I mean, when she goes out?"

Annie's eyes got wide. Emma hadn't noticed before how green her eyes were. "And not tell your mum, you mean?" Annie said.

Emma looked at her feet. "No. I guess . . . I didn't mean that," she said. Though of course, she had meant just that.

"We'll see about the papers later," Annie said. "We'll work something out. Now, away with you, all of you. Time for snacks. Tim, you help Emma carry Marmaduke and that cage to her room. Ira, you help Lizzie carry the tiger. And McClain, you hold me hand and be me helper. To the kitchen with all of you."

All five kids got up and began to trudge down the back stairs, with Woof leaping on ahead of them. Nobody followed Annie's directions, though. Instead, the twins grabbed Annie's hands. McClain trailed along behind, holding Tiger by the ear. Only Tim and Emma did what they were told. They took Marmaduke to Emma's room. Then they went back to the kitchen for their snack.

"Are you going to live here?" McClain asked, when they were all seated at the kitchen table.

Emma could tell that McClain hadn't quite made up her mind about Annie. Maybe it was because there was no sense in liking her if she was going to go away soon, like the other nannies had.

"Are you?" McClain asked again.

"Now, I don't know," Annie answered, handing

a bite of cookie to Woof. "I might. But then again, I might not. We'll see what your mum thinks after a time. What do you think?"

McClain just shrugged. "I think you talk funny," she said.

"McClain!" Emma said. "That's not nice."

"She does!" McClain said. "She says Mum."

"I can say Mum!" Ira said.

Annie just laughed. It was a deep, throaty kind of laugh, and suddenly, all the kids were laughing with her.

Emma laughed, too. She thought Annie might be the best nanny they had ever had, no matter how she talked. She looked at her brothers and sisters. They all seemed happy, even McClain. Emma felt a little happy place blooming inside of her, too.

"You know," Annie said, "I have me own mum. I visit her every Saturday."

"You do?" McClain asked.

"That I do," Annie said.

"But you're too old," McClain said. "I mean, to have a mum."

"Oh, no," Annie said. "No, you're never too old to have a mum. I love me mum just like you love your mum."

Just then, Mom came out of her office and into the kitchen, as the phone began to ring. Mom smiled at the kids and picked up the phone. Before she said more than hello, though, Emma knew: Trouble.

Mom's eyes got wide. She frowned. She looked at Emma. She shook her head. "Oh, my goodness," she said softly into the phone. "I'm so very sorry."

It was the school calling. No, it was Jordan's mom calling. Emma jumped up from the table.

Mom pointed at Emma. "Stay!" She said it silently, but there was no mistaking what she had said. Then she spoke into the phone some more, her face serious.

All five kids got quiet, looking from Emma to Mom, then back again.

"Are you in trouble?" McClain whispered.

Emma shrugged. She looked at Annie.

Annie's eyes were closed. Her lips were moving. It seemed that she was praying. After a moment, she opened her eyes and looked at Emma. "Oh, me dear, me dear," she whispered. "You wait and see. T'isn't much of a dilemma. The good saints, they never fail me."

Emma looked from Annie to Mom. She wasn't so sure of that. From the look on Mom's face, it wasn't a dilemma. It was a big, fat mess. And Emma didn't have to ask to know who was right in the middle of it.

Chapter Seven

Fire!

Emma was grounded for a week. No going out to play. And no computer games, either. Not even her Game Boy. Still, some really, really good things happened that week. Annie was going to live in. And Mom said Marmaduke could stay! Emma thought Mom changed her mind because Annie pointed out to her that if Jordan was squeezing the guts out of Marmaduke, then Marmaduke was only defending himself. Of course, Mom was really mad that Emma had sneaked Marmaduke to school, so that's why she'd been grounded.

But despite that, there was even more good news. Tryouts for the traveling soccer team were in a week, and Mom said Emma could try out. If she made the team, though, Mom said she had to continue to try and act responsibly. In other words, no more trouble! Emma promised. She loved soccer and was really, really good at it. Sometimes, she thought it was the only thing she was really good at.

So the Saturday after soccer tryouts, while Emma was still waiting to hear the results, she and the other kids got busy helping Annie move in and get settled. Usually, Saturdays were Annie's day off to go visit her mum, but this Saturday was different because it was moving-in day.

"What's Ireland like?" Emma asked, as she placed a picture on a shelf in Annie's little apartment. It showed a bunch of sheep munching grass outside a castle. "Are there really sheep and castles and stuff?"

"Indeed!" Annie said. "And fairies, too, if you're lucky enough to see one."

"Fairies aren't real," Tim said.

"No?" Annie said. "But me mother is real, and me dad, too. Now look at their picture here." Annie took a picture in a silver frame from a box. She rubbed the glass with a cloth and then turned it so the kids could see. Ira and Lizzie scrambled up onto her lap.

It was a photo of a pretty woman, holding a violin across her lap, and a man, standing behind her and smiling down at her.

"She's pretty!" Emma said.

"Is that your daddy?" McClain asked.

"Yes, though he's gone from us, died and went to heaven. And here's me sisters, all seven of them. And me mum with the fiddle. She could play so sweetly, it brought all the leprechauns out to dance."

"I don't think so," Tim said. "That's just folklore. And leprechauns are folklore, too."

"Really, now," Annie said. "And aren't you the fancy one for knowing such words?"

"It's true, though," Tim said, holding up the book he had picked up from Annie's stuff: *The Course of Irish History.* "It says right here that there's lots of folklore in Ireland."

"What's folklore?" Emma said.

"It means like stories, but they're not really true stories," Tim said.

"Well, there are plenty of stories that are true," Annie said. "Every Saturday when I go home to me mum, she has a new story for me. Someday, I'll tell you about the O'Malley fishermen. And someday, I'll even make you a stirabout! And tea and scones. Now where are you going, little rascals?" she asked, as the twins scampered down from her lap.

"I'm helping with pots," Ira said. He went to a box and dumped it over, spilling out plastic lids and bowls.

Lizzie picked up a bowl and put it on her head.

"Now aren't you grand!" Annie said. "Time, I think, to make me some tea."

She took a kettle out of a carton, filled it with water, and set it on the front burner of the stove. She didn't turn it on, though. She just stood there with her hands on her hips, thinking.

"Now what was I about to do?" she asked nobody in particular. And then she said, "Oh, I know. The milk and sugar for me tea. I'll be back." And she ran down the back stairs to the kitchen.

Emma went to the stove and fiddled with the knobs. They were a little different from the ones in their own kitchen downstairs. But then she figured it out and turned on the burner under the kettle. She smiled. She knew how much Annie loved her tea, and she'd be pleased to have her kettle "singing" when she came back upstairs.

"I wish I had a kitten," McClain said, her arm tight around Woof's neck. "I'd be really good to it. I wouldn't squeeze it like Jordan squeezed Marmaduke."

"Well, you're squeezing Woof hard enough," Emma said. "Now come on. We're supposed to be helping. You could pick up all those pots that Ira just knocked over."

"Not now," McClain said. "I got to put my bathing suit on. Woof and me will be back. Come on, Woof."

"Mom's going to be mad if you put on that bikini," Emma said. "It's too cold."

"Not," McClain said.

That's when Emma smelled something. She wrinkled up her nose. She sniffed. Burning. Something was burning. "Tim?" she said.

Tim put down his book. "It stinks," he said.

"It's burning, I think," Emma said. "Something's burning."

She looked at the stove. The burner was getting red under the teapot. But it wasn't burning. At least, it didn't seem to be. There was smoke, though. It was coming from the oven. But the oven wasn't turned on, was it?

The smoke alarm went off. Woof came bounding across the room. He began to bark. He braced his feet, so that his legs went all stiff.

"Stop it, Woof!" McClain said.

Woof didn't stop. He bounded across to the stove, then bounded back to them. That's when Annie came racing up the stairs. She looked around. She crossed the kitchen in two huge steps. She pulled open the oven door, grabbed a towel, and yanked out a tray. Then she tugged open the kitchen window, and the smoke alarm quieted down. "Oh, no!" she whispered. "Oh, no. Me passport, me precious passport."

All the children scrambled to look.

Emma eyed the smoking, charred mess on the tray. The edges of the paper were curling up, glowing red for a minute, then settling into ash.

Annie didn't speak, just shook her head slowly.

"I guess it's my fault," Emma said. "I thought I'd turned the burner on, not the oven. I didn't mean to . . . I was just . . . I mean . . . why is it in there?"

"To stay safe," Annie said.

"Oh," Emma said.

They all stared at the mess, even Ira and Lizzie, who were attempting to claw their way up Emma's legs to try to see better.

"In a fire, you should stop, drop, and roll," McClain said. "Like this." She dropped down on the floor and rolled over.

"I can do a log roll!" Lizzie said.

"Watch me!" Ira said.

"Uh oh," Tim said. "Mom."

They listened. Sure enough—footsteps, sharp footsteps, Mom's boots walking down the hall below them. Suddenly, the footsteps came more rapidly. "Kids? Annie?" Mom called. "Where are you? What's burning?"

Emma looked at Tim. Tim looked at Emma. They both looked at Annie.

"Kids?" Mom called again. "Something's burning! Where are you?"

"We're here, Mom!" Emma called. "We're coming right now."

"The fire's out!" McClain called.

"Hush!" Emma said to McClain. She turned to Annie. "Mom's going to be mad. But you can get a new passport, can't you?"

"I don't know, sweetheart," Annie said. "But I should've known better than to put it in such a place. Don't worry your head none."

But Emma's head was worried. Now Annie had no passport. And, what if Mom got rid of Annie because of the fire when it was really Emma's fault? But Emma couldn't admit to that, not with soccer season coming up. Could she?

Chapter Eight

Emma Tells

As soon as they had finished lunch and the twins were put down for their naps, Mom called Annie into her office and shut the door.

Emma and Tim and McClain stationed themselves outside the door. Mom probably didn't know it, but everything that was said in her office could be heard in the hall.

Emma was more than a little worried. She knew how fast Mom hired and fired nannies. Most times, Emma didn't care. But Annie was kind of special. At lunch, Annie told all the details of what happened. Emma watched Mom's face when Annie told about the passport in the oven. Mom looked like she had just swallowed a kitten.

Emma had kept sending signals to Annie, shaking her head and motioning her to be quiet. But Annie just went on and on. She told about how wonderful the kids were, smelling smoke, doing their drop-and-roll thing. She even bragged about how brave and true Woof was. And she didn't say a word about who had turned on the stove. Emma wanted to speak up and tell the truth—she really, really did. But the words just wouldn't come out of her mouth. Besides, she thought, it wasn't turning on the stove that was the problem. The problem was the passport being in the oven—right?

Now, Emma was sure that Mom would lecture Annie about how serious it was to let something burn up in the stove. Emma pressed her ear against the door.

Sure enough, Mom was saying, "Five children! And if they had been trapped up there . . ."

"Every family should have an escape plan for a fire or emergency," Annie interrupted. "Does your family have one?"

"Well, no," Mom said. "I don't think we've ever done that."

"Shall we plan one then?" Annie said.

"Well, yes," Mom said. "I guess we should. But about this morning . . ."

"And you really should have a rope ladder up there," Annie said. "Why without that, if the stairs were on fire, there'd be no way out."

Emma giggled and put a hand over her mouth. She grinned at Tim. He grinned back.

"Annie's so smart," Emma whispered.

"I was smart, too, right?" McClain whispered.

"You were smart," Emma whispered back. "Now hush."

"Want to see me drop and roll now?" McClain whispered.

"No! Not now. Hush. Listen," Emma said.

But there was nothing more to hear. Mom had moved out of earshot. All they could hear now were some muffled sounds.

They all retreated to the front hall then, waiting for Mom to come out. McClain stretched out flat on the hall rug, her head resting on Woof's back, her eyes drooping. In a minute, Woof was asleep. Emma thought that soon McClain would be, too.

Tim picked up his skateboard, sat on the stairs, and looked at his watch. "I wish they

would hurry up," he said. "I want to go out."
The rule was that no one could go outside
without asking Mom or Annie first.

Emma wanted Mom to hurry up, too, so she
could ask permission to practice soccer with
Luisa in the park. Even though tryouts were
over, she needed to practice in case she got
chosen. Any day now, the letter would come,
telling if she had made the team.

Emma started bouncing the soccer ball
back and forth from one knee to the other.
She was getting pretty good at controlling the
ball. Here in the hallway, she was extra careful because of things like the big mirror and
the grandfather clock. Once, the ball got
away from her and bounced off the mirror,
but only lightly. Emma retrieved it and was
about to do a header, but thought better of
it. She looked at Tim, who was looking at his
watch again.

"I'm supposed to meet José at school in five
minutes," he said.

"School? Why school?" Emma asked.

"We use the ramp at the side by the soccer
field. We jump from the ramp to the steps,"
Tim said. "You should see how good we are."

"I know," Emma said. And then she had a thought. She tilted her head and looked at Tim. "How come you're not scared of skateboards?" she asked.

"Skateboards?" Tim asked. "Why would I be scared of skateboards?"

Because you're scared of everything, Emma thought. But of course she didn't say that. "No reason," she said. "But I am. You know that."

That was the truth. Last year, the first time Emma tried Tim's skateboard, she fell and broke her wrist. Still, she tried skateboarding again the very same day that the wrist cast came off. That day, she broke her elbow. But she never did tell Mom how she'd done it.

"*You*, scared?" Tim said. "You're not scared of anything."

Emma shrugged. She really couldn't think of much that scared her, but she didn't want Tim to feel bad, either. So she just said, "I'm scared of a couple of things."

"Know what I'm scared of now?" Tim asked.

"What?" Emma said.

"That Mom will fire Annie," Tim said. "That she'll send her away today, maybe."

Emma sighed. "I know," she said. "I'm scared of that, too."

"I know what to do," McClain said.

They both swiveled their heads to look at her. She wasn't asleep at all. She was sitting straight up and had heard every word they said. "I'll say I did it," McClain exclaimed.

Emma smiled at her. "I don't think so, McClain. You're too little. If Mom thought you touched the stove, she'd—I don't know what she'd do. Make you eat dog food or something."

"She would not," McClain said. And then her face got kind of scrunched up. "I don't want Mom to be mad at Annie."

"Don't worry, Clainie," Emma said, using her pet name for McClain. "It'll be all right." She took a deep breath. She stood up. She looked at Tim. "I'm doing it. I'm going to go in and tell."

"You are?"

Emma nodded.

"Okay," Tim said, setting down his skate-board. "I'll go with you."

"You will?" Emma said.

"Sure," Tim said.

"Me, too!" McClain said, scrambling to her feet.

Emma looked at her brother. She looked at her sister. She smiled. "Okay," she said. And all three of them marched down the hall and into Mom's office. Emma didn't even knock.

Chapter Nine

Annie's Locked Out

When Emma got home from school on Monday, she saw the letter she had been waiting for. It said "U-Nine Soccer" on the envelope—Under Nine—kids under nine years old! It lay on the hall table with the other mail. Emma thought she'd burst with excitement. She snatched up the envelope and raced to the playroom at the back of the house. Had she made the team? And if she had, would Mom let her play? Mom hadn't been too mad about the fire, especially because, as Annie kept pointing out, Emma had owned up to the truth. And it hadn't been her fault that the passport was in the oven. Even Mom knew that. Still, Emma had been on her best behavior, and now, here was the letter!

"Annie, look!" Emma cried, bursting into the room. "It's here. My soccer letter."

But Annie wasn't there. Nobody was there.

"Hey, Annie!" she called. "Where are you?"

No answer.

That was odd. Emma stopped and thought. Today was Monday. Monday, Tim had computer after school, and the little kids—oh, yes! Monday, McClain had dance in the early afternoon. That meant all the little kids had gone down for their naps afterward. So they were probably still in bed. But where was Annie? She wouldn't leave the kids alone.

"Annie!" Emma called again, but more quietly, so she wouldn't wake up anybody.

Still no answer.

She ran to the bottom of the steps that led to Annie's apartment above. She opened the door. "Annie?" she called softly.

Nothing.

She shrugged. Well, maybe Annie was just in the bathroom. She'd wait a few minutes and then call her again.

Emma ran upstairs to her room, the letter still in her hand. She didn't dare open it because it wasn't addressed to her. It was addressed to

Mr. and Mrs. O'Fallon—Mom and Daddy. Still, she thought there might be a way to see what it said inside. She plopped her books on her desk and closed her door. Then she let Marmaduke out of his cage so he could play a little and held the letter up to the light.

Nope, she couldn't see through the envelope. Still, it *had* to be her invitation to play on the traveling team. But then she had a bad thought. What if the letter just said, sorry, maybe next year?

Ohmigosh, Luisa! Had Luisa made the team? Emma ran to her computer. She knew that Luisa checked her e-mail *every* day after school.

While Emma's computer was warming up, she changed out of her school clothes.

She put on her sweats and soccer shirt, the long-sleeved one because it was a little cold out. She was just about to sit down in front of the computer, when she heard some strange thumping sounds. Hammering maybe? She tilted her head, listening.

Yes, there was a definite thumping sound. It came every few seconds. Thump. Thump. Thumpity-thump. Thump. Thump. Thumpity-thump! Woof scratching? No, it was way too loud for that. And where was it coming from?

Emma got up. She opened her door, then went out in the hall, listening. Yes, there it was again—that thumping sound. It seemed to be coming from—where? In one of the little kids' rooms?

She went down the hall to the twins' room and opened the door, quietly. Both babies were in their cribs, napping peacefully. They hated naps. But ever since Annie had come, they happily took naps for her, maybe because she sang them to sleep. For a moment, Emma watched them. Ira had one arm tight around Puppy, his stuffed rabbit. Lizzie's face was all pink and sweet, her hair in little sweaty curls all around her face.

Quietly, Emma closed the door and then went down the hall to McClain's room. She tried the knob, but the door was locked. McClain sometimes ran to her room and locked her door after she'd had one of her tantrums. Mom and Daddy kept a key hidden on the ledge above the door where McClain couldn't reach it.

Emma stood on tiptoe, got the key, and unlocked the door. Even unlocked, the door was hard to open, and Emma thought she knew why. Sometimes Woof settled himself against the door. Sure enough, when she eased the door open, she had to push Woof a little bit. He looked up, then scrambled to his feet.

"Hush, Woof!" she said.

She looked around. There was McClain, sound asleep in her bed, scrunched up in one little corner. All of her dolls, dozens of them, were lined up carefully on the pillows so there was hardly any room left for her at all.

Well, that was weird. McClain was napping. Ira and Lizzie were napping. But no Annie. Why would Annie leave the kids alone?

That's when Emma heard the sound again, that knocking sound, much louder, much closer. She looked around. And almost died of fright. There, at the window, peeking in—a face. Annie's face! Annie was perched outside on a ladder!

Chapter Ten

More Trouble

Annie mouthed something to Emma.

Emma hurried across the room. She shoved the curtain aside and pushed up on the window. It took a bit of pushing and tugging, but after a moment or two, the window slowly creaked upward. "Annie!" she said, leaning out. "What are you doing out there?"

"Trying to get in," Annie said.

"Why?"

"Well, it's a *wee* bit cold out here, for one thing," Annie said.

"I mean, why are you out *there*?" Emma said. "I mean. . . ?"

"Give me a bit of a hand, will you?" Annie said. She put her hand in through the window,

and Emma took it. "I'll just work me way in—
if I can stay free of these tree branches and
not knock down the ladder."

Emma held Annie's hand, as Annie came
up another step of the ladder. Then, when
Annie was up high enough, she leaned her
shoulders in through the window, resting her
elbows on the windowsill.

"Just let me catch me breath," she said.
"And I'll climb right in."

"What happened?" Emma asked.

"McClain locked the door, because I wouldn't
let her wear her bathing suit," Annie said,
looking over at the bed where McClain was
just beginning to stir. "And here, it's almost
winter! Little rascal. I couldn't leave a wee one
alone in a locked room, now, could I? But I
was having a bit of a problem pushing this
window up."

"Annie," Emma said. "McClain locks the
door all the time! The key is up on the ledge
above the door. Didn't Mom show you?"

Annie shook her head. "If she did, I don't
remember," she said. "But I don't think so. Now
let's see if I can't get me-self in here." She put
both hands firmly on the window ledge, then

looked down at Woof, who was pacing back and forth under the window. "And Woof, you stay out-a-me way," she added. "I'm comin' in."

"Okay, Woof!" Emma said. "Out of here."

"Why's Annie out there?" McClain said suddenly.

Emma turned. McClain was scrambling down from the bed. "Can I go out in the tree, too?"

Suddenly, there was a huge commotion in the tree just behind Annie's head. A squirrel scurried up the tree trunk, flew onto a branch behind Annie, and skittered across it, so close it was almost in Annie's hair. Another squirrel followed with its tail flicking back and forth wildly. They chattered and squeaked, and Woof lunged at the window. His front paws scraped against the windowsill as he thrust his head outside. Annie and the ladder swayed madly.

"Woof!" Emma cried.

She shoved him aside, reached out, and tightly grabbed Annie's hand, which was frantically clinging to the window ledge. Annie's other hand was whipping around behind her, trying to catch onto anything.

"Hold on, I got you!" Emma yelled. She leaned her entire upper body out the window and gripped Annie's free hand. Annie's feet were firmly on the ladder, but it was still swaying wildly. Slowly, with Emma pulling, the ladder tilted toward the house and then swayed back toward the tree again. Emma kept her hold on Annie's hand as fiercely as she could. Then finally, finally, the ladder tilted forward enough to rest against the house. Emma and Annie were face to face at last, just inches apart on either side of the window. They panted and stared at each other in shock.

"I think I can get me-self in now," Annie said. And, after just a minute of resting, she did just that. She crawled up over the windowsill, scrambled in, got her feet on the floor, and straightened her clothing.

"Why were you in the tree?" McClain asked.

"Oh, you little rascal child," Annie said, bending down to McClain. She hauled McClain up and into her arms. "Don't you ever lock your Annie out again, understand?"

"I won't," McClain said. "Are you going to tell Mum? I mean, Mom? Please don't. Can I go out in the tree?"

"No, you cannot," Annie said. She turned

and looked at Emma. "You saved me life," she said.

Emma shrugged.

"Oh, but you did," Annie said. "Wait 'til I tell your mum and dad!"

And then they looked at one another, Annie's eyes wide. Emma thought she knew what Annie was thinking. If Annie told Mom how responsible Emma was, that would mean telling on McClain. Yet, Emma would love for Mom to know about her bravery. The soccer letter was here. Still, Emma had a feeling that Mom wouldn't much like the idea of Annie trying to climb through the window.

"I don't think you need to tell," Emma said. But she said it so softly that she wasn't sure that either Annie or McClain heard.

Chapter Eleven

Chaos

The letter was an invitation for the traveling team! And Luisa had gotten one, too. The only problem was that Mom said she and Daddy still had to think about it. They had lots of things to consider—like Emma being responsible enough for such a thing. Also, there would be an informational meeting for the parents on Saturday morning. Mom said they'd have to wait until then to decide.

"Why can't you decide now?" Emma asked when they sat down to dinner. "I've been really responsible, haven't I?" She thought about that afternoon. Nobody had said anything to Mom about it. And the more Emma thought about it, the more she was sure it was best to keep quiet.

Mom and Daddy would have a fit if they knew about Annie and the ladder.

Emma looked over at McClain and then back at Daddy. He had just returned from his second trip to Ireland in two weeks, and they were all having dinner together for the first time in a while.

"Daddy, Marmaduke hasn't escaped in weeks, ever since Annie got him his new cage," she said. "And I've done my home-work. And I've helped Annie with the twins and I've . . ."

"Emma!" Daddy said. He reached across the table and took her hand. "You are a great kid. You really are. Mom and I have noticed that you've acted more responsibly lately. But there are other things to consider. Who will drive you to all the places where you'll be playing? How often? What will it cost? And how about all the practices during the week? Let's just wait and see. On Saturday we'll have all the information we need to make a decision. Right?"

"Wrong," Emma said. She stuck out her lip. She knew there wasn't any use arguing, though. Mom and Daddy wouldn't decide 'til they got all the facts. That was just the way they were. *Get all the information and then make a decision. Just wait and see.* Mom and Daddy said that a hundred times a week. It just about drove Emma crazy. But at least Daddy had noticed her good behavior.

Still . . .

Emma looked across the table at Tim who had started in on Daddy again about what he wanted for his birthday. For some reason, she suddenly felt mad at Tim, even though she knew it was silly. He wanted an iPod. He'd begun telling Daddy all the reasons he should get one, and Emma felt like she was hearing one of those courtroom arguments on TV. How could he be so organized like that, even inside his head? He'd probably get his iPod, too! And she had to *wait and see!*

She tuned him out and watched Ira and Lizzie trying to eat with chopsticks. Emma saw Ira's sippy cup of milk teeter on the edge of his tray.

"Watch it!" she said. She reached and caught it just in time.

"Thanks, Emma!" Mom said. She shook her head. "Annie comes up with the oddest things. I don't know why she went and bought these chopstick things for them."

Emma knew why. It was because the twins had been fighting over the one set of chopsticks they already had. Annie just went to the Chinese restaurant down the street and got more sets so the twins would stop fighting. Emma had to agree with Mom, though. With the chopsticks, the babies were making even bigger messes than usual.

"Everywhere I look, I see Annie's strange effect on this household," Mom went on, but she was actually smiling. "Like McClain. A couple of weeks ago, she'd only eat applesauce and mashed potatoes." Mom turned to McClain. "Now, you're a regular little gourmet. Imagine liking scones and tea!"

"I like scones," McClain said. "With raisins."

Well, maybe she did, Emma thought. But right now, it didn't seem that she liked her dinner much. She was only picking at it.

"Know what?" McClain said. "Annie said if I keep trying new foods, she's getting me a hamster for my birthday."

"Oh, no, she's not!" Mom said.

"Is, too," McClain said. "She promised."

"We'll see about that," Mom said.

"She keeps promises," McClain said. "Today

she was mean, though. She wouldn't let me wear my bikini."

"A good decision," Mom said. "It's fall!"

"It's not cold," McClain said. "I was mad at her."

"Well, I don't think you had any right to be angry at her," Mom said. And then she squinted her eyes at McClain. "Did you go to your room when you got mad?"

McClain nodded.

"And then what?" Mom asked. "You didn't lock Annie out of your room, did you?"

McClain didn't answer.

"McClain?" Mom said. "Did you? How many times have I told you about that?" Mom looked over at Daddy. "I hope Annie remembered . . ."

"She didn't," McClain said. "She had to climb in the window."

"She had to *what*?" Mom said.

"Climb in my window. She couldn't get in, though. But Emma . . ."

McClain suddenly stopped. She looked at Emma. "Oh," she said.

"Oh?" Daddy said.

"Oh, *what*?" Mom said.

"Oh, nothing," McClain said. She kept on looking

at Emma. "I mean, nothing! Right?" She looked back at Daddy and lifted her shoulders, like she was trying to shrug, like there was nothing wrong. But the longer Daddy looked at her, the more McClain looked guilty. At least, that's how she looked to Emma. And when Emma looked at Mom and Daddy, she had a feeling that they thought so too.

Emma's heart thumped hard. "Mom!" Emma said. "Mom, about that soccer letter. Can we. . . ?"

Mom put up her hand. "No, we cannot," she said. "What did Daddy just tell you? We have to wait 'til Saturday. Now, I want to hear the rest of what went on this afternoon." She turned to McClain. "McClain?" she said.

McClain did that innocent look again.

"McClain? You locked the door?" Mom asked. "And Annie climbed in through the window?"

"Emma helped," McClain said. "But it was hard because of the squirrels in the tree. And Woof."

"The squirrels?" Daddy said. "And Woof?"

"Woof wasn't in the tree," McClain said. "Just the squirrels."

Mom turned to Emma. "Emma?" she said.

Emma tried to make her face blank, the way Daddy did when he didn't want to answer something. "What?" she said, trying to look all innocent. She hoped she was better at it than McClain.

"Why didn't you tell us about this?" Mom said. "Didn't Annie remember where the key was?"

Emma shook her head. "She said she forgot."

Mom took a deep breath. Emma could see that she was hopping mad. Her face got as red as McClain's. She turned to Daddy.

"I just don't understand Annie!" she said. "I just don't. One minute she's so responsible. The next minute, you'd think she was a child herself." She turned back to Emma. "And you! How could you not tell me something so important?"

Emma shrugged.

"Annie climbed up a ladder into the house?" Mom said. "What if she had fallen down? What if something terrible had happened and—?"

And at just that moment, something terrible did happen. Marmaduke came racing into the dining room, his little silver body almost flattened to the floor, slithering under chairs and around corners, with Woof behind him, yapping like crazy.

"Emma!" Daddy cried. "Catch that creature!"

Emma jumped up from the table. She raced after Marmaduke, reaching under Mom's chair, but he got away. She ran around the table and blocked him as he headed toward the kitchen. She scooped him up and held him tight. She had forgotten that she'd let him out of his cage when she got home. And with all the excitement, she had never put him back in.

"Oh, Marmaduke," she whispered. "I'm sorry. I forgot." And to Woof, who was still leaping at her and at Marmaduke, she said, "Cut it out, will you? Now go! Sit down."

"That's it!" Mom said. "I've had it with that animal. He has to go, cage or no cage."

"No!" McClain wailed, her face getting even redder. "That's mean. You can't send Marmaduke away." She started to pound her little fists on the table.

"McClain, are you getting sick?" Mom asked suddenly. She put a hand on McClain's forehead. "Why, you're burning up!" she said. She looked across the table at Daddy. "She's sick! She's got a fever."

"I do not!" McClain said. She slid down from her chair. She stood beside Mom, her fists resting on her hips. "Everybody's being mean to me and to Annie and to Emma and to Marmaduke!" she said. Suddenly, she bent over. And just like that, she threw up. Right into Mom's lap.

"Yuck!" Emma cried.

"Gross!" Tim said. He pushed back from the table.

Daddy jumped up, hurried around the table, scooped up McClain, and rushed her into the bathroom. Emma could hear McClain throwing up again. She hoped that this time it was over the sink or toilet.

Mom stood up, holding her skirt away from her. "Emma, Tim!" she said. "Watch the twins, will you? I have to change." She raced into the hall and upstairs.

Emma looked down at Marmaduke, then over at Tim. "I forgot I let Marmaduke out before," she said.

"If only Woof didn't have to chase him all the time," Tim said. And then he said, "Watch it!" because Ira had knocked his sippy cup to the floor.

"Clainie threw up," Ira announced. He looked kind of sick, too, maybe just from seeing the mess.

"I can throw up," Lizzie said.

"Don't you dare!" Emma said.

"I won't," Lizzie said.

"I . . . I . . ." Ira said. His eyes got wide and round, and suddenly he looked really, really pale. "I do," he said. And just like that, he threw up in a neat little pile right there on his highchair tray.

He looked at Tim. He looked at Emma, and he began to whimper.

"Daddy!" Emma called. "Ira threw up!"

Daddy came back into the dining room with McClain in his arms. Gently, he set McClain down on a chair. Then he went to the high-chair and unbuckled Ira. He lifted him away from the mess. "Here you go, buddy," Daddy murmured to him. "It's all okay. It's all, all okay."

And Emma hoped, she really, really hoped that Daddy was right about that. Because with Mom's announcement about Marmaduke getting sent away, nothing seemed right at all.

Chapter Twelve
Saving Annie

The twins were finally cleaned up and bathed—Lizzie had thrown up, too—and now they were asleep in their beds. Mom said it was probably just a stomach flu. Emma hoped like anything that she wouldn't catch it, too. She hated throwing up. McClain was asleep, too, sprawled out in the middle of Mom and Daddy's king-sized bed. Whenever McClain got sick, she got really, really high fevers, and so Mom kept her in their bed to keep an eye on her. Mom and Daddy were sitting on the little sofa at the far end of their bedroom where the TV was. Emma and Tim were sitting on the floor. They weren't there to watch TV, though. Emma had been called in for a "talk." Tim had come along to keep Emma company, and Mom and Daddy didn't seem to mind.

"Emma," Mom said, speaking quietly, so as not to disturb McClain. "McClain did something she's been told not to do. She locked herself in her room. It was wrong, yes, but she's not even five years old yet. When something like that happens, we need to know about it."

Emma sighed and looked down at her fingertips. She'd been chewing on her nails again, and she tried to hide them from Mom by balling her hands into little fists. She was glad nobody on the soccer team cared about fingernails.

"So why did you keep that a secret?" Mom asked.

Emma shrugged. "Because it wasn't a big deal," she said. "McClain locked Annie out. Annie didn't know about the key. So she got a ladder and climbed up to the window. So?"

"So?" Mom said. "So we know that. But why didn't you tell us?"

"I don't know!" Emma said. "I guess 'cause I thought you might get mad at her. Even though she was only trying to help."

"You're right," Mom said. "We are mad at her. But I'm really upset with you, too. Haven't we been talking about responsibility lately? Is it responsible to keep a secret like this? And on top of that to let Marmaduke get loose again?"

Emma didn't answer. But she was thinking plenty: *There goes my soccer team. And there goes Marmaduke.* She felt a fat lump grow in her throat. But she couldn't give up without a fight.

"Marmaduke got out because . . . well, because I heard Annie at the window, and I went to help so I forgot I had let him out of his cage. And anyway, it's not like anything bad happened to Annie."

"You're right, it didn't," Mom said. "But it could have. What if Annie had fallen off the ladder and laid there on the ground with no one around to help?"

"And then you all would have been all alone in the house," Daddy added.

"Well, that didn't happen," Emma said. "So I don't understand why you're making such a big deal about it!"

"Because Daddy and I worry about you children," Mom said. "And, I'm afraid to say, we worry about Annie."

"What do you mean, you worry about Annie?" Emma glanced at Tim, then turned back to Mom. "Annie's the best. I think it was very responsible of her to not want McClain locked up in her room alone."

"I don't know, Emma," Mom said. "Daddy and I aren't so sure about Annie. First, the fire, and now this."

Emma and Tim exchanged worried looks.

"You're not sending Annie away, are you?" Emma asked.

Mom and Dad looked at one another.

"No!" Emma whimpered, tears jumping up to her eyes.

"No!" Tim cried, his eyes welling up with tears, too.

"How can you do that for . . . she was trying to help. And about the fire—it was just an accident!" Emma cried.

"Grownups aren't supposed to have that kind of accident," Daddy said. "They're supposed to pay attention."

"Grownups have accidents, too!" Emma said, and she could feel tears spilling over her eyelids. "You have accidents! You ran over a cat once. You told me."

Daddy put his hands to his head.

"And if you're still mad about today, think about the key," Emma said. "Are you sure you told Annie about it? She doesn't remember that you did. And she's only been here for, like, three weeks, maybe four. Up 'til today, McClain hasn't locked her out once! That means . . ."

"It means you kids like Annie," Daddy interrupted. "It doesn't mean she's responsible."

Emma took a deep breath. She opened her mouth to speak. She closed her mouth. Well, heck, she wasn't going to be allowed on the soccer team anyway. And she couldn't let them send Annie away. She might as well say it. But she hesitated for just another second.

"Mom? Daddy?" she said, finally. "You know why we like Annie? We like her because she's nice. She's responsible, she really, really is, no matter what you say. And she's honest. And she's fun. She would have told you tomorrow about the ladder and the door and all, you know that. I don't think she needed to, but I know she would have. You guys fire every single nanny we get just because they're not perfect. And, well, nobody's perfect.

I'm not, and she's not, and . . ." Emma paused. Oh heck, why not? "And *you're* not!" she added.

Mom was frowning. "Emma . . ."

"And you know what else?" Tim said, leaping to Annie's defense, too. "You should have taken the lock off McClain's door. That wasn't very responsible of you."

Daddy sighed. "I know," he said. "I tried. But I couldn't get it off. Not without ruining the door."

"So, ruin the door!" Emma said.

"And know what else?" Tim said. "Did you notice how Ira and Lizzie take naps now? Did you know Annie—"

" —sings them to sleep," said Emma, finishing his sentence for him. "She sings them Irish lullabies."

Daddy didn't answer, just did that holding-his-head-in-his-hands thing again. Emma took that as a good sign.

Tim must have, too. "It's not fair to expect people to be perfect," he said. "Everybody makes mistakes."

Nobody said anything more for a minute.

Daddy looked at Mom. "I think it's fair to say

that Annie gets another chance, don't you?"

Mom threw up her hands. "I give up," she said. "You win."

"You mean that, really?" Emma said.

"Really," Mom said.

"Good!" Emma said. "Promise?"

"Promise," Daddy said.

"Don't be mean to her tomorrow, okay?" Emma said.

"Why would I do that?" Daddy said.

"Well, I mean, you're going to have a talk with her, right?"

Daddy looked at Mom. "Probably," he said. "But don't worry. You can trust us. We know the whole story now."

Well, thought Emma, not the *whole* story. But she felt a whole lot better. She looked at Tim. He gave her a high five. They both stood up.'

"'Night," Emma said.

"'Night," Tim said.

"'Night," Mom and Daddy said.

But at the door, Emma had another thought. She turned back. "Mom? Daddy?" she said. "Marmaduke? It's all right about Marmaduke? I mean, you're not going to . . ."

Mom laughed. She shook her head, and then she laughed again. "Emma," she said. "Marmaduke is a mess. He'll never stay put no matter how many cages we get for him. But he's part of the family, I guess, so he can stay. Maybe I was just being a little harsh."

"Really?" Emma said.

"Really," Mom said.

"For good?"

"For good!"

"Annie, too?" Emma said.

For just a minute, Mom hesitated. Emma was almost sure Mom was going to say yes. But she didn't. Instead, she just said, "Get!" and she waved a hand at Emma. "Now go to bed. Quick. Before I change my mind."

Chapter Thirteen
The Biggest Problem of All

It was Saturday. Nobody was throwing up anymore. Mom and Daddy were going to the soccer meeting. Annie's mom had gone back to Ireland for a long visit, so Annie was taking care of the kids even though Saturday was her usual day off. They all went to the huge town playground and from there, the library. Tim had heard that somebody was giving a talk about a new Einstein book, and he wanted to get it. By late afternoon, everybody was tired and ready to go home. The twins fell asleep in their stroller. And McClain got so sleepy that Tim and Emma took turns pushing the stroller so Annie could carry her.

They turned the last corner toward home. It was almost dark, even though it was only five o'clock, and the street lights were winking on. As they walked past the dry cleaner's shop, Emma studied the flyers posted in the window about the upcoming soccer tournament. She hoped like anything that she'd soon be part of it.

Up ahead, Emma could see their house. The porch lamp lit up the front steps, and all the lights were on inside the house. It made Emma happy, seeing the lights turned on like that. She didn't know why, exactly. But she loved seeing her home. And the lights at night made it seem even more special.

Just as they were going up the steps, the front door opened, and Daddy came out with Woof on his leash.

"Hi, Daddy!" Emma yelled. "What happened at the meeting? Can I walk Woof with you?"

"Sure, Sweetie," Daddy said. "Come on." He smiled at Annie and the kids. "Tell Mom that Emma's with me, okay?"

"Me, too?" McClain said, lifting her head from Annie's shoulder. But then she plopped her head back down, and Annie carried her into the house.

As soon as Emma and Daddy were on their way, Emma asked, "What happened at the meeting? Can I be on the team?"

Daddy was quiet for a long time.

That made Emma worry.

"Well," Daddy said finally, "it was interesting."

"Yeah?" Emma said.

"Very interesting," Daddy said. "Very expensive, too."

"I could use my allowance."

They had reached the park, and Daddy unsnapped Woof's leash. Woof galloped off.

"I'm afraid it would take more than your allowance," Daddy said. They went on into the park and sat down on a bench near the entrance.

"How much more?" Emma said. "I have some money saved in my bank."

Daddy smiled at her. "Do you have a thousand dollars?"

"A thousand dollars!" Emma said. "It costs a thousand dollars?"

"Well, not quite a thousand, but eight hundred. That includes hotel and travel," Daddy said. "And insurance and fees for the games."

"Wow," Emma breathed. "I didn't know that."

A thousand dollars! That was like, like, well, she didn't know what it was like. But since she got five dollars allowance a week, she knew she couldn't come up with that much, not even if she saved for an entire year—two years, maybe ten years! And there was no way she could expect Mom and Daddy to pay the whole thousand dollars.

She leaned back against the bench. Her heart fluttered away like a little bird. She felt tears creep up to her eyes. She blinked them back.

"So I can't be on the team?" she said after a bit.

"I didn't say that," Daddy said. "See, your mother and I really, really want you to be on the team."

"You *do*?" Emma asked.

Daddy nodded.

"How come?"

"Because you've acted more grown up lately. You've become more responsible. And we want to reward you."

Emma smiled. She thought about all the good things she'd done, like saving Annie's life—though she hadn't told Daddy about that. But she couldn't help thinking of some of the bad, like sneaking Marmaduke off to school and . . . She didn't say anything.

"And so, a thousand dollars or eight hundred dollars is a lot of money," Daddy went on. "But it isn't quite out of our reach. There's a bigger problem, though."

At that, Emma sat up straighter. What could possibly be bigger than a thousand dollars? If they could do that, they could do anything. "What?" she asked, suddenly feeling a whole lot better.

"I've looked at my flight schedule," Daddy said. "There are eight away games for the team you'd be on. I'm going to be gone for four of them. The rule is that every child must have a parent or guardian for each away game. No exceptions."

"So?" Emma said. "Mom could go."

"And the little ones?" Daddy said.

"Oh," Emma said. And then she said, "That's easy. Annie."

"Annie's off on Saturdays, you know that. Today was an exception. She just did it because her Mom's away and so we could go to your soccer meeting."

Emma flopped back against the bench again. She'd think of something. She would. There must be a way.

"Well, let's wait and see," Daddy said. "Mom and I thought maybe we could hire somebody else for Saturdays."

But Emma didn't want them to hire somebody else. That was what had happened with other nannies. The new ones seemed so good

91

that Mom would let the old ones go. And then she eventually fired the new ones, too.

"So tell me about your day at the park and the library," Daddy said.

"It was fun," Emma said. But she wasn't really paying much attention. She had a lot to think about.

"What did you do?" Daddy asked.

Emma shrugged. "The usual. Ira made me push him on the swings 'til my arms almost fell off. Lizzie had to chin herself on everything. And McClain found worms. You know how she loves worms. But she held them so tight they died, and then she cried."

Daddy smiled.

"Oh, and you know what else?" Emma said. "We went to the library, and there was someone there talking about Einstein." She looked up at her dad. "Did you know that Einstein made lots of mistakes?"

Daddy shook his head. "No, I guess I didn't know that."

"Well, he did," Emma said. "Some people think he spent the last half of his life chasing something foolish."

"And what was that?" Daddy asked.

"Something about matter and everything being the same. Or something," Emma said. She really hadn't understood it herself. But she did remember one thing she had learned.

She stood up and called for Woof. She always got a little nervous when he was gone for long, especially in the dark. She heard him galumphing toward them from the other end of the park. He was panting and huffing and making little woofing sounds. When he got close to her, she snapped his leash on, then turned to Daddy.

Daddy reached out and took her hand, and they turned toward home.

"Know what Einstein said that was funny?" Emma asked.

"What?"

"He said that anyone who has never made a mistake has never tried anything new," Emma said.

She thought of the new things she had tried lately. And she thought of the big mistakes she had made. And then, for some reason, she found herself telling Daddy all about the other day and how she had saved Annie from falling out of the tree. She told about how the ladder swayed and about reaching out, and about how it took all her strength to pull Annie back to safety.

Maybe it was because Annie was always so honest that Emma felt the need to tell. Or maybe it was because she figured that Annie would tell anyway. Or maybe it was because she was really kind of proud of it. At first when she started talking, Daddy seemed very serious. But then he started to laugh. Then he laughed even harder. Finally, he was laughing so hard, that it made Emma laugh, too. She hadn't really thought about how funny it was, especially the part about Woof trying to get into the tree. By the time they were back home, both of them were still giggling.

Emma looked up at him as they started up the steps. "So it's all right then?" she asked. "You think I did okay?"

"Of course you did okay," Daddy said, grinning down at her. "You were very smart and responsible and so was Annie. I even think . . . well, maybe you even saved Annie's life."

"That's what Annie said, too," Emma said.

Daddy put an arm around Emma's shoulder and pulled her close. "But Emma," he said softly. "Maybe we don't need to tell your mom about this, okay?"

Emma looked up at him and nodded. "Okay by me!" she said.

Chapter Fourteen
Emma's Solution

When Emma got home with Daddy and Woof, Annie was in the kitchen, perched on the high stool at the counter. She was talking while Mom peeled carrots. Emma had never seen them chatting like that before. She wondered if they were becoming friends.

Tim was sitting on the floor, his back against the pantry door, buried in a book. The little kids were watching a *Baby Mozart* video in the corner of the kitchen where there was a tiny TV set and VCR. Their eyes were wide open. They leaned toward the screen, even though they'd seen the video a thousand times before. When the dragon popped up, McClain put her hands over her eyes like she always did. She said she wasn't afraid of the dragon. Still, she always covered her eyes until the dragon was gone. Emma kind of understood. That dragon coming up close to the screen and sticking out its tongue *was* sort of scary, even to a big kid like herself.

"Hi, sweetie!" Mom said, as Emma came into the kitchen. "I hear you learned about Einstein at the library."

"Yeah," Emma said.

"Was it fun?" Mom asked.

Emma shrugged. "Einstein made lots of mistakes," she said. And she wondered why she kept thinking about that. Maybe because it felt good that important people made mistakes, too.

"Annie's going to have supper with us tonight," Mom said.

"She is? I mean, you are!" Emma said. She threw her arms around Annie and hugged her. Emma always begged for Annie to stay and eat with them. But Annie always said no. At the end of the day, she said, she needed to go home—even though her home was only in the apartment upstairs.

"How come?" Emma said. "I mean, I'm glad, but . . ."

Annie and Mom exchanged looks.

Uh oh, Emma thought.

"Annie's a bit unhappy tonight, I think," Mom said.

Emma turned to Annie. "You are?" she said. "I mean, are you?"

Annie shrugged.

"Don't be sad," Ira piped up from the corner of the room. He scrambled to his feet and came and leaned his head against Annie's knee. "It's o-tay," he said.

Annie leaned down and scooped him up. She held him close to her, snuggling her face into his neck. Then she lowered him to the floor, and Emma thought she saw tears in Annie's eyes.

Emma felt her heart thud heavy inside her. Annie had been fired! She was leaving them! That's what this was all about. Mom had changed her mind about the tree and the fire, and she'd fired Annie. But she was letting them have one last dinner together. Maybe Annie had told about almost falling out of the tree, just like Emma had told Daddy, and Mom realized how dangerous it was and . . .

"Annie?" Emma said.

Annie just shook her head. She was blinking hard.

Emma looked across the room at Tim. He had looked up from his book at her. They each sent a signal to the other with their eyes.

Do something!

But what?

"Mom! It was *my* fault!" Emma burst out. She looked at Daddy. "Whatever happened, it . . ."

"No, it was mine!" Tim said, scrambling to his feet. "I could have . . ."

"No, really!" Emma said. "If I'd been . . ."

"Whoa!" Mom said, putting down the carrot and the peeler and holding up both hands. "It's nobody's fault. Nobody did anything. What's with you two? Annie's just a little sad, that's all."

Emma looked at Annie. "How come?" she asked. "You weren't sad all day."

Annie shrugged. "Maybe I was. A little," she said.

"Why?" Tim asked.

"I miss me mum," Annie said. "I guess I even miss Ireland sometimes."

Oh. That was all?

"But your mom, she's coming back soon, right?" Emma said.

"Not soon. Not for three months."

"Three whole months?" Emma said.

Annie nodded. "It's too expensive to go abroad for a short visit. So she's going to stay for three months and visit her sisters and her aunties. Today was the first weekend. I guess I feel a teeny bit lonely, is all."

Three months. Three whole months of weekends.

The whole winter soccer season.

Emma looked at Mom, her eyes wide.

Mom shook her head, like she knew what Emma was thinking.

"But Mom!" Emma said. She turned to Daddy.

Daddy frowned and looked from Mom to Annie and then to Emma.

But again Mom shook her head. "Annie works only five days a week."

"But it's not *work*!" Emma said. She turned to Daddy. "Right, Daddy?" she said.

Annie was looking from one to the other.

"What's not work?" Annie said.

"Taking care of all of us!" Emma cried. And even with Mom frowning at her, Emma told about the traveling soccer team. And about parents or guardians.

"I could do that," Annie said. "I'd like to do that. Me brothers played soccer in Ireland a long time ago. I did, too, as a girl. Only there, we called it football."

"You never told me that!" Emma said.

"Well, I stopped playing," Annie said. "I broke me ankle twice and . . ."

Annie stopped. She tried to look innocent but was as bad at doing that as McClain was. "But it healed fast," she said quickly. "It's all better. Me pet pig was the mascot."

"Did he have a name?" Emma asked, trying to head off Mom and Daddy thinking about broken ankles.

"Who? The pig?" Annie said. "Yes, his name was Archibald. Does your team have a mascot?"

Emma shook her head. "No. But sometimes somebody gets dressed up in a bear costume. That's all. Because our team name is the Bruins."

"Maybe Woof could be your mascot," Annie said. "When he doesn't have a haircut, he looks like a bear."

"Now, Annie," Mom said. "Don't be giving her any ideas."

"Like anyone has to," Daddy murmured.

"Where'd your mascot go?" Emma asked.

"Oh," Annie said, shaking her head. "Christmas came, and Archibald was gone."

"Gone? Gone where?" Emma asked.

Annie frowned. "I think somebody killed him. They ate him."

"They *did*?" Emma said.

"Really, Annie," Mom murmured, frowning at her.

"But that's awful!" Emma exclaimed.

"Well, they were hungry," Annie said. "And he was a pig. Still, it surely made me sad."

"Annie," Mom said. "Let's talk about something else. Now, you don't have to do this. We're been talking about hiring someone else for Saturdays. I'd like to be free to go to Emma's away games. . . ."

"Oh, no," Annie said. "Let someone else take care of *my* children?"

Mom just raised her eyebrows.

"Who else could we trust them with?" Annie continued. "I mean, you have five little ones here. Even without Emma, that's four, and they're quite a handful, I can tell you. Why just the other day when I was locked out . . ." She trailed off.

Emma closed her eyes.

When she opened them, Daddy was looking at her. He smiled.

"I think we should let Annie do it," Daddy said. "She wants to, and Emma can't be on the

Patricia Hermes

team unless we find someone else to look after the kids. Annie is surely reliable enough."

Mom looked at Daddy, like he had suddenly sprouted a carrot from the top of his head.

"Really," she said.

"Really," Daddy said.

Mom just shrugged. "Well, if you think so." She turned to Annie. "We'll pay you, of course."

"That's settled then," Emma said. And before anyone could change their minds, she jumped up and threw her arms around Mom and Annie. "Oh, I love you guys!" she said.

And then she ran to Daddy. "I love you, too," she whispered. And she gave him the biggest hug of all.

Chapter Fifteen
A Pretty Much Happy Ending

Emma lay awake for a long time that night. She had taken Marmaduke out of his cage and brought him into bed with her. She snuggled him close. Some nights, Marmaduke just rustled around and couldn't wait to get away. This night, though, he seemed content to snuggle.

For a long time, they lay together, Emma breathing in the sweet, musky smell of Marmaduke's fur. "What do you think, Marmaduke?" she whispered to him. "Is Annie the best or what?"

Marmaduke snuggled into her armpit, his nose rooting around, looking for a way to crawl into her sleeve.

"Stop it, rascal," she said. She moved him away. "Just think! I can be on the team. But now I'm sad for Annie, missing her mom and all."

Marmaduke slid his head under Emma's chin, snuggling close. It seemed like he felt bad for her, too. He stayed still for a while. Emma slid her hand up and petted him. His thick, strong fur felt rough, but nice, beneath her hand. "We'll have to find a way to make Annie happy. Okay?"

She could tell from his breathing that Marmaduke was falling asleep. Emma wrapped her arms tight around him and closed her eyes. She thought of what she and the kids could do. A party maybe? Bake her a cake? Make a present for her? Draw her a picture?

When she opened her eyes later—how much later?—it was very dark. She looked over at her clock. Midnight. She felt under her chin. Marmaduke was still there, sleeping warm against her. He felt so warm and snuggly. It made Emma feel safe. And happy.

And that's when Emma knew just what to do for Annie. Annie could borrow Marmaduke! She could sleep with him and snuggle up, just like Emma was doing. Marmaduke was the best for cheering you up—especially if someone had eaten up your pet pig. That had made Emma really, really sad.

Quietly, she slid out of bed. She pulled on her robe. She remembered about putting on her frog slippers. Then, she scooped Marmaduke up in her arms and tiptoed down the hall. She stopped just outside Tim's door. He had changed his computer screen saver. Now it had stars and moons floating around in a deep, green sky.

Emma watched it a moment. It was really pretty. Who would have thought of a green sky? She wondered why God hadn't made the sky green. That would be a funny thing. She'd have to ask Annie. Annie seemed to know a lot about God.

She was still looking over her shoulder at the screen as she started toward the stairs. That's when she stumbled, tripping over Woof asleep at the top. She threw out her hands to catch herself.

And then Woof wasn't asleep anymore. And Marmaduke was no longer in her arms. He was skittering down the stairs. Woof was racing after him. Woof was also woofing. His deep, heavy bark echoed in the still house.

Oh, no! Emma felt her heart thudding hard inside her. She closed her eyes and took a deep breath. And then she went racing down the stairs, not even bothering to skip the steps that creaked. Behind her, she heard Mom and Daddy's door open.

She heard Daddy call out. "Emma? Is that you?"

"Yes! It's . . . it's us!" she called back.

At least this time, she thought, she had remembered to put on her frog slippers.